Dear Parent:
Your child's love of reading starts here!

Every child learns to read in a different way and at his or her own speed. Some go back and forth between reading levels and read favorite books again and again. Others read through each level in order. You can help your young reader improve and become more confident by encouraging his or her own interests and abilities. From books your child reads with you to the first books he or she reads alone, there are I Can Read Books for every stage of reading:

SHARED READING
Basic language, word repetition, and whimsical illustrations, ideal for sharing with your emergent reader

BEGINNING READING
Short sentences, familiar words, and simple concepts for children eager to read on their own

READING WITH HELP
Engaging stories, longer sentences, and language play for developing readers

READING ALONE
Complex plots, challenging vocabulary, and high-interest topics for the independent reader

ADVANCED READING
Short paragraphs, chapters, and exciting themes for the perfect bridge to chapter books

I Can Read Books have introduced children to the joy of reading since 1957. Featuring award-winning authors and illustrators and a fabulous cast of beloved characters, I Can Read Books set the standard for beginning readers.

A lifetime of discovery begins with the magical words "I Can Read!"

Visit www.icanread.com for information on enriching your child's reading experience.

For Ezzy and Levon

JiNX   SpiKE   Spot   MaX

I Can Read Book® is a trademark of HarperCollins Publishers.

Library of Congress Control Number: 2015932002
ISBN 978-0-06-235703-8 (trade bdg.)—ISBN 978-0-06-235702-1 (pbk.)

The artist used Adobe Illustrator to create the digital illustrations for this book.
Design by Martha Rago. Hand-lettering by James Horvath.

James Horvath

Dig, Dogs, Dig

A Construction Tail

Duke   Roxy   Buddy

HARPER

An Imprint of HarperCollinsPublishers

4

Wake up, dogs.

You're going to be late.

The sun is up.

There's no time to wait.

Grab your gloves,

hard hats, and boots,

shovels, goggles,

and dirt-digging suits.

Hop in your trucks.

There's work to be done.

Get to the job site.

Run, dogs, run!

Down the road
and over the hill,
driving big trucks
takes plenty of skill.

Around the corner
and through the pass,
stop at the station
to fill up with gas.

Okay, dogs.

We're at the site.

There's a lot to do

before it is night.

Jump in the dump trucks,

and graders and loaders.

Buckle your seat belts

and fire up the motors.

Here comes the digger
with its metal scoop,
pulling up dirt
with a swish and a swoop.

Push and plow
and clear the way—
the bulldozer makes it
look easy each day.

The loader picks up
a rocky big bite
and moves out the rubble
with all of its might.

Hauling the dirt,
gravel, and rock,

the big, strong dump truck
works round the clock.

"There's trouble in the pit.

We've hit something big.

Get down in the hole and

dig,
dogs,
dig!"

Down in the pit

there's some busting to do,

with hammers, a pick,

and a rock splitter, too.

A job like this
calls for a crane,
with its big, strong hook
and its long, heavy chain.

It's a dinosaur fossil,

a huge T. rex bone!

With a tug it breaks loose

from its very old home.

Now get back to work.

Get back to your crew.

Hurry up, dogs.

There's more work to do.

The graders smooth out

the uneven ground

by scraping and pushing

the earth all around.

The cement mixer spins

as the concrete pours,

but there's no time to waste.

We're going to need more.

Building has started.

Here come more big trucks,

hauling plants and trees

and even some ducks.

More dogs arrive with

last things to do,

adding fountains and benches,

and painting them, too.

Everything's finished.

What a day this has been.

Now open the gates
and let everyone in.

The workday is over.

It's now almost dark.

We have just enough time

to enjoy our new park.

Great work, crew. It's
a place all your own.
There's even a spot
for that dinosaur bone!

This job is complete.

We've built something new.

Tomorrow we'll find

a new job to do.